Postman Pat's
Christmas Tree

Story by **John Cunliffe**

Pictures by **Joan Hickson**

From the original Television designs by **Ivor Wood**

André Deutsch/Hippo Books

Published in hardback by André Deutsch Limited
105-106 Great Russell Street, London WC1B 3LJ
and in paperback by Hippo Books,
Scholastic Publications Limited
10 Earlham Street, London WC2 9RX

ISBN 0 233 98450 X (hardback)
ISBN 0 590 76187 0 (paperback)

It was cold and snowy in Greendale. Christmas was coming. Pat had more and more letters and parcels to deliver each day. All the people of Greendale were busy, getting ready for Christmas.

When Pat called at Greendale Farm,
Mrs. Pottage was making mince-pies.
"Have some mince-pies," said Mrs.
Pottage.
"Just one, please," said Pat. "I don't
want to get fat."

At the school, the children were making streamers and calendars.

"Where is Lucy?" said Pat.

"Poor little Lucy," said Mr. Pringle. "She slipped on the ice and broke her leg, last night. She's in Pencaster hospital."

"Oh, dear," said Pat, "that's unlucky, at Christmas. She'll be missing some of the fun. I'll pop over and see her when I've finished my round. See if I can cheer her up."

The children gave Pat a big card and a present to take for Lucy.

Lucy was delighted to see Pat. He told her all the Greendale news, and made her laugh with his jokes. Then he went round the ward to have a chat with the other children.

"Dear me," said Pat to the nurse, "they haven't got many books and toys, have they? It must get a bit dull for them."

"We just haven't got the money for books and toys," said the nurse. "I wish we had."

"We'll have to see what we can do," said Pat.

All the way home, Pat was thinking of ways to raise money for the children at the hospital. And as he went on his round the next day, he asked the people of Greendale.

"We could have a special collection in church," said the Reverend Timms.

"I'll make some cakes for the Christmas Bazaar," said Dorothy Thompson.

"We could have a raffle," said Miss Hubbard. "I'll give three bottles of my best rhubarb wine."

Everyone wanted to help.

On Wednesday the wind got up, and that helped more than anything else, as you will see. It blew a big fir tree into the road, not far from Greendale Farm. Pat couldn't get past with his van, so he went to get Peter Fogg, with his tractor and power-saw. Peter was just going to cut the tree up and drag the pieces away, when Pat had an idea.

"Hang on, Peter," said Pat, "do you think we could move that tree all in one piece?"

"We could with the big tractor," said Peter, "but it'll be a lot easier to cut it up."

"No, don't do that," said Pat, "that tree's given me an idea. It's a Christmas-tree! We could put it up on the village green and get Ted to rig some lights up. Then we could have a special carol concert, and a Christmas Fair in the village hall. Lots of people would come from the towns to see it, and we'd raise plenty of money for the hospital."

They had a real old time moving that
tree to the village green. It took two
tractors and a trailer in the end. A lot
of people came to help, and PC Selby
diverted the traffic.

Colonel Forbes brought a huge tub to put the tree in. Ted borrowed a JCB to lift the tree into place. The tree looked lovely, but there was still a lot to do.

The children at the school made decorations to go on the tree, and posters to advertise the carol concert and Greendale Christmas Fair.

Ted began fixing up the lights. Then he said, "Why don't we have lights on the church, and the post-office, and the village hall, as well?"
And he went off to Pencaster to borrow more lights.

"It's going to be better than Blackpool Illuminations," said Pat.

"We mustn't get carried away," said Miss Hubbard.

Everyone began making extra cakes, and mince-pies, and Christmas puddings, to sell at the Christmas Fair.

Granny Dryden's knitting needles were going at top speed, making tea-cosies and dishcloths.

Miss Hubbard made a special flower display in the church. It was lovely.

There had never been such a busy Christmas in Greendale.

Ted arranged special bus trips to Greendale, from Pencaster and Carlisle.

The Pencaster Gazette had a big article on the front page, with a picture of Ted putting the lights up, then they put in free advertisments for three weeks. There was even an article in a colour magazine, on Sunday, with a whole series of photographs, headed:

GREENDALE PREPARES FOR A SPECIAL CHRISTMAS

"We'll have to have a celebrity, to switch the lights on," said Mrs. Goggins.

"We have our own celebrity," said
Mrs. Pottage. "Everyone knows Pat.
He'll have to do it. It was all his idea,
after all."
Everyone agreed with that.

The Big Day was a week before
Christmas. Lancaster Silver Band
came to play for the carols. The
Mayor of Pencaster came to switch the
lights on. And crowds of people came.
There was even a special train from
London. Miss Hubbard had to make
several extra trips with the Greendale
bus to collect everyone. Radio
Pencaster came with their radio car, to
report live from the scene.

All was ready. The Mayor made a speech.

"Keep it short," whispered Ted. "It's too cold to hang about."

The moment came to switch the lights on. Pat stepped forward, and pressed the big switch. There was a loud bang, and a splutter, a flash, and a cloud of smoke. The lights flashed on for a moment, then went out. The crowd said:

"Ooooooh!"

Then:

"Aaaaaaah!"

It was a good thing Ted had his tool-kit handy.

"It's blown a fuse," he said. "Don't worry, I'll soon fettle it."

And he did.

The lights came on.

The band played.

The choir sang.

The crowds joined in. They filled the church for the service. They filled the village hall for the Christmas Fair.

They filled the collecting-boxes for the
hospital. It was wonderful. A
Christmas to remember for years and
years afterwards.

When all the money was collected and counted, there was more than enough to fill the children's ward with books and toys. The rest was given to the hospital funds. After that, children had a much nicer time in hospital, thanks to the tree that blew down, and Pat's bright idea, and all the people of Greendale who joined in to help.